Paperback ISBN: 979-8-9947638-0-3

First edition, 2026

Cover and interior illustrations by Serinnarie

Published by Fox & Sock Studios

Printed in the United States of America

PROLOGUE: Before The Students Arrive

Spirits fell in sequence as three soldiers in royal blue advanced in practiced formation. When the last spirit dissolved into fading resonance, the unit regrouped. One soldier keyed the radio at his hip, cycling channels until the static cleared.

"Third <u>Rapid Response Detachment</u> to Overwatch," he called in flatly. "Area secured."

"Acknowledged," came the reply. "Good work, Operator Diaz. Return to city hall before sunrise. Over."

Diaz clipped the radio back onto his vest and adjusted his grip on the rifle as the squad moved away from <u>Academy</u> grounds.

"Third one this month," he whispered under his breath.

A squadmate scoffed. "B-tier. And none of them are in the reports."

Diaz frowned. "We sweep the perimeter daily before students arrive."

He waited to check the response of the other two soldiers.

"Doesn't sit right."

Re:Wind

Before Tomorrow

By 5IVE

Table Of Contents

The squad leader stopped immediately, staring at Diaz with eyes that gave warning.

"You don't say that."

"I'm just— shouldn't we at least inform—"

"You're not saying anything," the leader cut in. "Orders come from the Capital. From the Premier himself. We execute them."

Diaz went quiet as they squeezed through the bushes and trees. Pylons came into view, their inactive frames marking the edge of the zone.

"Almost out of this maze," the rear soldier muttered. "I hope our detachment isn't called in tomorr–"

The forest cracked as a tree tore sideways through the air. The rear soldier vanished beneath pine branches and leaves.

"Captain! There's the spiri—"

Without saying a word, the Captain placed his hand above the muzzle of Diaz's rifle, not allowing him to take aim.

"No," the Captain said with a stern voice.

Diaz stared in confusion, "Sir?"

"Students are on campus now," the Captain said. "We will have to brush this one under the rug. Tomorrow's detachment will handle it."

The Academy disappeared behind them as they reached the road. By morning, no report would mention the tree or the fallen soldier.

CHAPTER 1: Holding It Together

The academy halls were too quiet for a place built to train students for war. Outside, the <u>Union's</u> flag waved under The Academy's flag. Inside, sunlight stretched through tall windows and settled across glistening stone floors. Stella's footsteps echoed down the empty hall. Five centuries of victories reduced to names and dates, each inscription preserving an outcome The Academy had already approved. Stella passed beneath them, slowing down when she saw the gold name plate that was too big to ignore.

DEVIGNE LEGACY

"This is their version of success," Stella said under her breath.

Stella instantly flinched, almost colliding with a passing student. The papers slid from her grip and scattered across the floor.

"Sorry about that."

Stella crouched, gathered them, and aligned the corners. She continued on her way, staring at the pages in her hand to avoid the awkward moment.

Temporary Vice President.

The word stood alone on the header. A role The Academy had always maintained, now altered to include an expiration.

"Temporary," Stella muttered.

"No."

Stella straightened her posture, smoothed her expression into something neutral and calm, and turned the handle. The door swung open.

"Good morning!"

The voices of the council members hit her all at once. The council room was already full. The air felt warmer inside than in the halls, pleasantries continuing as she entered.

An orange-haired girl with an athletic, slender build sat sprawled casually across one of the chairs. Her boots crossed at the ankles, far too comfortable for someone who outranked the room in combat evaluations despite being the lowest-ranking member. She glanced up first, eyes sharp and immediately amused.

Beside her was a lean boy with bangs covering his eyes, hands in his pockets, expression relaxed.

Near the window was the final figure. A boy with his posture straight and hands folded behind his back, exactly where he was supposed to be.

"How was your morning?" The orange-haired girl said brightly, her tone just a little too sweet. Her green eyes closed as her lips formed a grin. "We were worried you overslept."

Yumi Lumiere.

The girl who became ranked one, even without noble blood.

The boy with bangs, Kai Claremont, chuckled. "Overslept? Her? Not a chance."

Stella was already aware he'd never once questioned whether he belonged here.

The most confident of the group inclined his head slightly. "You're right on time."

Cedric Pentaguarde.

The perfect student who leads this student council. He wasn't raised here and somehow fit better than anyone, as if the room adjusted to him.

Stella snapped out of her thoughts and nodded while forcing a small smile as she stepped fully into the room and shut the door behind her.

"Oh good," she said while taking tiny steps forward. "I stopped by the front desk for the reports."

She held the papers up like proof, immediately aware of how unnecessary it was.

Yumi's grin widened. "Always reliable, you make the rest of us look bad."

Kai didn't even look at her. "You do that on your own."

"Hey!" Yumi shot back, twisting in her chair. "That's not... okay, maybe a little."

Cedric laughed quietly as Kai instantly joined in. Yumi protested louder, half-serious, half-playing it up. Stella waited for the moment to pass so she could speak again. She was close enough to be included by proximity, but distant enough to feel like an interruption.

Just hold it together.

CHAPTER 2: Where The Rain Waits

"Guys—it's happening! The rain, it's not touching anything!"

The interruption came without warning. The door burst open as chairs were still scraping into place. A student, now breathless, stood in front of the council.

Stella was already on her feet. Kai looked at the student and lifted his hands. "Slow down. Start from the top."

"It's raining all over campus," the student declared, words tumbling over each other. "But it just—stops. Before it hits the ground. Before it hits anything."

Cedric stood up, leaving his papers on the table. "Show us."

They spilled into the hall and down the stairs. By the time they reached the courtyard doors, Stella could already feel it. A pressure in the air that didn't belong to weather. The courtyard looked unreal. Rain filled the sky but never landed. Droplets hovered inches above stone paths, railings, and rooftops, remaining suspended and unmoving. A few students reached up instinctively, fingers passing through nothing. Faculty weren't here yet, that alone made Stella's chest tighten. The rain wasn't making a sound. Not a single drop hissed.

"Under the covered walkway," Cedric ordered. "Now."

Students clustered beneath the overhang. Cedric and Kai stepped forward, scanning the area. Stella knew the moment she stepped past the overhang, this would stop being an observation and start being a violation that could not be explained away as curiosity or instinct. She walked straight into the courtyard, away from the covered walkway.

"Stella," Kai spoke sharply, already tense.

She ignored him, moving slowly across the cement and onto gravel near the grass line. The air grew colder the closer she got. The rain hovered inches above her shoulders, close enough to feel, but never touching.

"That spot," Stella uttered, quietly.

Yumi glanced at her, arms crossed. "Wow. You're really committed to this, huh?"

Stella didn't respond to the comment and squatted next to the faint glow.

"Cedric," Reyna murmured from behind him, her voice uncertain but steady. "There's... there's a story." She hesitated, glancing around like she wasn't sure she should be saying it.

Cedric turned. "Go on."

"...about a boy. He wished the rain wouldn't stop. So he wouldn't have to walk home alone. The rain listened and granted the wish, but ended up holding in place as a response. That's how the story goes. Or—how people say it does."

Silence settled as the spirit revealed itself, at least to Stella. It was no longer human.

It took the form of a snail, timid and hidden, holding the rain in place from fear of letting it go. Its shell was fractured in places, light leaking through the cracks as it trembled, trying to keep everything from falling at once.

"He's not blocking the rain," Stella declared. "He's holding it."

Cedric's jaw tightened as he looked at Stella. "Faculty will clear this." His tone left no room for alternatives.

Stella stood abruptly, "I know." She turned and ran.

"Stella!" Kai called, unsettled now.

"If they get here first," she said over her shoulder, "they won't ask what it wants. They'll end it."

She pushed through the doors and returned moments later, breathless, with an umbrella clenched in her hands.

"Devigne!" someone shouted.

She ignored them as she knelt beside the spirit again, slowing her breathing.

"You shouldn't be alone," she said softly. "You didn't do anything wrong."

Stella hesitated as her grip tightened, "this could either free him or crush him."

She opened the umbrella. For a second, the rain froze completely. Then the fall began, uneven at first, droplets slamming too hard against stone before settling into something natural. The droplets began to regulate themselves, feeling real again. The spirit shimmered, then faded, finally free to move on.

Reyna exhaled, "I think... you reached him."

"Or she almost made it worse," someone muttered. "That's how incidents escalate."

Stella closed the umbrella and sat back on her heels, heart still racing. A few late droplets struck polished leather shoes far across the courtyard as a man approached.

"Devigne," he asserted evenly. "You acted outside council protocol."

Stella opened her mouth to respond, but her motion was met with his index finger pressed against his lips, signaling her not to speak. He paused, eyes flicking briefly to the umbrella still clenched in her hand.

"Effective immediately," he continued, tone unchanged, "your access to council-restricted archives and incident records is suspended for thirty days."

Stella's breath caught.

"You will retain your position," he added without looking at her. "This restriction applies only to sensitive materials. Temporary positions carry temporary privileges."

He glanced at the wet pavement already beginning to dry.

"Procedure exists precisely so results don't excuse deviations."

He turned and walked away, recording the incident without looking back. Stella stared at the ground long after the rain slowed.

CHAPTER 3: Good Morning, Reyna

The sun was barely rising when Stella walked to campus. She left her dorm early today, barely fixing her hair before slipping out the door. Her red bow held on by habit rather than placed with care.

"I wonder what Reyna will get for breakfast today," Stella thought as she walked, staff resting in her right hand while backpack hung loosely from her left shoulder. Reyna always insisted on choosing, always made a point of paying, and Stella decided she wanted to be the one to do it today.

"She always treats me," Stella murmured quietly, a faint smile forming despite the nerves she hadn't managed to shake since waking up. "This one's on me."

The morning air brushed against her face as she crossed the path toward the campus grounds, wind tugging at loose strands of her hair. As she approached the campus, she felt a strong presence of resonance in the air, then it vanished completely. The sound of metal penetrating wood was faint, but very clear.

The campus was still empty, students barely arriving from behind her. Stella hesitated, fingers tightening around her staff before she turned toward the forest line bordering the Academy ground.

She moved carefully, pushing past hanging vines and low branches, cautious and prepared, her steps measured as the foliage swallowed the path. From deeper within the trees, she caught sight of movement far away. Three blue silhouettes retreating through the greenery, already pulling away from the area. Stella opened her mouth, instinctively calling out.

"Hello?" Her voice didn't cover the distance. The figures faded between the trees without slowing, without reacting.

As the forest opened slightly, Stella noticed a dark splash of red against the grass that caught her eye immediately. Her steps slowed again as she approached it, her breath catching somewhere between disbelief and dread. For a moment, her mind refused to put shape to what her eyes were seeing. Her eyes felt deceiving as she saw the Academy uniform painted in red.

It was still intact, the fabric torn but recognizable, the academy insignia stained dark. Stella's gaze traveled upward before she could stop herself, and when she reached the face, her stomach turned violently. The features were almost unrecognizable, crushed as if caught between overwhelming force and the ground. There were no bullet wounds on the body.

"Reyna..." Her vision blurred as she staggered back, one hand bracing against the trunk of a nearby tree as her body reacted. Stella's grip on her staff released as she vomited against the trunk of a fallen tree.

Stella tore back toward the Academy, stumbling over roots and vines, catching herself on branches as she pushed forward, knees scraping hard against the ground when she tripped and forcing herself up again without stopping. Her knees, now bruised and bleeding. By the time she reached the school grounds, only a handful of students had gathered near the entrance, their expressions confused as she rushed past them and burst through the council doors.

"Cedric! Yumi! Kai!" Her voice cracked as she called out, lungs burning as she fought for air.

"Guys— please— come with me."

The three members rushed quickly. Whatever they'd been doing was abandoned instantly as they followed her back outside, weapons, bags, and papers left behind without a second thought.

"What happened?" Cedric asked as they ran.

"I didn't expect to be sprinting this early," Yumi muttered, trying for humor, but the words fell flat as her eyes caught Stella's face. Blue liquid streamed down Stella's cheeks, forced backward by the wind, her expression empty in a way Yumi hadn't seen before.

"Over here," Stella managed, turning toward the forest again.

"Over he—" Stella was at a loss. The body of Reyna was no longer there. Nor the uniform, staff, or backpack Reyna had with her. The only thing that remained was the grass, stained red at the spot she was in.

"Reyna... she was right here," she commented quietly, the words barely forming. Stella collapsed to the ground with her face toward the floor.

The three of them stared in silence, the weight of the absence settling in. Kai was the first to speak, his voice in defeat.

"We'll report it," he declared. "The Academy will—"

Yumi didn't let him finish. She stepped closer to Stella, placing a steady hand on her shoulder as Cedric continued to look down at the ground, his jaw tight. He remembered Reyna's voice from the day before, telling him about the boy in the rain, the way she'd spoken so softly.

"Yumi," Cedric said after a moment, not looking up. "I need you to handle the report. This one is..." the words couldn't come out as he was stricken with grief.

Yumi nodded her head as she helped Stella back up from the ground. Stella tried to use her staff with trembling hands, trying to detect life forms, but there were none present, not even resonance residue remained. Eventually, they turned back toward the Academy, walking slowly this time, heads lowered, the morning continuing around them as if nothing had happened. Stella drew a sketch of Reyna in first period, unable to forget her best friend.

CHAPTER 4: The Garden

The student council decided to meet at the Academy's community garden for the rest of the week. There was no announcement made about Reyna, but the council wanted to pay their respect. The sun sat high overhead, beating down on the rows of flowers and vegetables. The four wore bamboo hats to keep their face from the heat. Swords, snipers, and staffs were left behind and in their place were shovels, hoes, and watering cans.

"I'm beat," Kai announced, pausing to lean on his shovel. He wiped sweat from his cheek with his forearm "I didn't think it would take this long."

Stella knelt near the edge of one of the plots, using a hand trowel to loosen the roots. "It always does," she said as she routed weeds out.

Cedric worked in silence a few rows over, adjusting the spacing between plants where they'd been set unevenly. Yumi was making a mess of her section. Dirt clung to her gloves and sleeves. Her shoes filled with soil that made her stop to shake her shoes. The crew worked in silence.

Stella shifted closer and continued digging. As she brushed loose dirt aside, something small moved near the edge of the plot. A snail crawled slowly across the ground, the shell shone from the sunlight. Stella paused to watch it for a moment, remembering that snails were Reyna's favorite animal.

Kai noticed she wasn't moving across the rows as she was previously. "You good?"

Stella nodded at Kai and went back to work. A few minutes passed in silence. The only sound for the next passing minutes were gravel being moved and water pouring out of the spout.

"If only there was a way to buff your gardening skills–" Kai started, then paused at the thought. He exhaled and adjusted his grip on the shovel. "Nevermind."

Yumi glanced up at the comment, but didn't give input.

They worked until the sun began to dip and the shadows stretched longer across the soil. The rows weren't perfect and some plants still leaned off-center. A few clusters of flowers remained unfinished. Near the edge of the garden, Stella placed a small wooden signpost. She carved a simple drawing into it earlier that day, careful not to rush the lines. A drawing of Reyna she made earlier the week.

They stood side-by-side for a moment, hats now tucked under their arms. Cedric brushed the dirt from his hands and looked over the garden.

"We should head back," he suggested. "Tools need to be returned before the shed closes."

They all nodded as Stella grabbed the wagon to put the tools in. As they walked away, Stella glanced back to the garden. The snail was still there, inching its way along the damp soil. One of the watering cans sat forgotten beside the plot, but she didn't turn back to get it.

Stella's drawing of Reyna Lewis, Third Year

Student

The Academy

CHAPTER 5: Normal

The first sign something was wrong didn't come from an alarm. The council room shuddered beneath their feet, just enough to rattle the papers on the table. Chairs scraped as everyone shifted at once. A low thud echoed throughout the building, followed by a sharper vibration that traveled up the walls like a pulse. Stella's head snapped up towards the source.

Cedric was already standing. "That wasn't structural," he asserted, calm but alert. "That came from above."

Another impact hit somewhere overhead as glass shattered. Still, no alarms sounded. No pylons flared. The intercom stayed silent. That absence made Stella's stomach drop.

"Class B," Kai hypothesized slowly, eyes narrowing. "That's where the vibration localized."

Yumi's grin sharpened. "Huh. Guess something slipped surveillance."

Cedric grabbed his weapon. "Move."

They were out the door before the echoes finished fading. Boots hit the stairs hard as they took them two at a time. The lights dimmed automatically for after-hours, shadows stretching long across the walls. Stella felt the resonance halfway up.

Definitely above D-tier, she thought immediately.

The pylons should've caught this.

Stella felt the thought lock into place, cold and immediate. The outer sensors would have flagged it first, then the midline, then the outer ring.

Nothing triggered.

Offline systems left traces through partial alerts or mismatched readings. There had been none of that. The pylons must have been prevented from responding.

"Overwatch didn't flag anything?" Kai asked, breath steady despite the pace. "They'd have to cross three layers of pylon detectors before even seeing the academy."

Yumi laughed under her breath. "Guess today's special."

They reached the entrance of Class B just as another impact struck from within. The doorframe splintered, dust shook loose from the ceiling tiles.

Cedric raised a hand, "Formation." They moved without question.

Cedric took center, hand resting on his hilt, stance grounded. Yumi slid to the left, already angling for line-of-sight, her sniper coming up smoothly. Kai shifted behind her, sigils threading instinctively into place as he began reinforcing output and perception.

Stella stepped in last. She positioned herself opposite Yumi, staff in hand, off-angle from Cedric. The resonance responded immediately as she began to channel mana. She was close enough to cover him, but kept distance to avoid crossfire. A thin form of resonance gathered along the staff in controlled layers as she began shaping a containment field, keeping it shallow enough to deploy instantly without interfering with Cedric's movement.

Faculty would arrive, as they always do for internal breaches.

This wasn't a live-fire zone nor was it a tournament. This was supposed to be classified first.

The classroom door burst inward. Desks lay overturned, chairs shattered against the far wall. Papers drifted through the air like ash. At the center of the room stood the spirit. Humanoid in shape, but wrong in every detail. Its form pulsed unevenly, resonance leaking from fractures along its torso. It twitched as it turned toward them, movements jerky and unfocused.The spirit did not advance. Its posture remained fixed, resonance output fluctuating in short, uneven pulses that never fully stabilized.

Stella's barrier pulse tightened.

"It's confused," she told herself. *"If it escalates, I shield. If it stabilizes, I will contain it. Either way, I'm ready."*

Cedric stepped forward. "Now-"

The words barely left his mouth as Yumi moved. She broke formation in a single fluid motion, vaulting over a fallen desk as her scope snapped into alignment. Kai's buff flared automatically, threading into the bullet in the chamber before Stella could react. The shot cracked through the room.

The spirit didn't recoil, but shattered. Resonance bloomed outward violently, then collapsing in on itself. Fragments dissolved as they hit the air. The pressure vanished so fast it left Stella dizzy.

Her barrier started, but had nothing left to contain. Silence slammed down.

Yumi landed lightly, straightening as if she'd just finished stretching.

"Huh," she said lightly, rolling her shoulder. "Didn't mean to steal that," she shrugged and grinned easily. "Haven't fought something real all year."

Cedric exhaled and sheathed his blade. "No worries," he replied reassuringly. "Threat neutralized."

Stella realized no one had looked at her once.

Kai chuckled. "That leap was insane. Cleanest shot I've seen this semester."

"One more tally for the board," Yumi added, closing her eyes as she smiled. "Guess I was overdue."

Stella didn't move. Her staff hummed faintly in her grip, resonance dissipating unused. She stared at the empty space where the spirit had been, trying to reconcile the stillness with what had just happened.

It hadn't attacked. Her body had already prepared to shield, and now there was nothing left to contain.

Footsteps echoed somewhere down the hall. They weren't close nor urgent.

Cedric gestured toward the door. "Let's report and clear out."

The footsteps arrived at the doorway. Faculty.

An administrator stepped in, gaze sweeping the room before settling on the damage. His gaze lingered briefly on Stella's staff, still charged.

"Report will list this as a D-tier escalation," he informed flatly. "Contained internally, with no external alert."

His attention stopped on Stella. "You hesitated," he concluded with confidence. "And hesitation was unnecessary."

The word landed heavier than the tremors. Stella opened her mouth, but the words stayed at the tip of her tongue.

"Yes, sir," she let out, looking down at the floor.

The administrator nodded. "Replacement planning will be addressed during your review next month."

He turned and left without another glance. The room felt colder after that.

The council filed into the hall. Yumi stretched, hands lacing behind her head. Kai was already talking about something else, the tension evaporating from his voice. Cedric walked ahead, posture unchanged.

Stella followed last, her staff felt heavier now, as she walked out with her head down, following the feet of the others.

The response had followed procedure exactly.

And for the first time, she wondered whether the system allowed space for anyone who refused to act without legitimacy.

Chapter 6: Visible

The classroom felt stuffy as the fifth period began. Stella sat two rows from the front with her notebook open. She wasn't taking notes yet, her mind wasn't on the lecture. She was distracted by yesterday.

A torn-up classroom. Glass on the floor. A spirit who is no longer a spirit. And Yumi. The way she'd moved like she'd been starving.

"Oops, didn't mean to take your kill." The words stayed with her.

Stella pressed her pencil down until the tip snapped.

"Idiot," she mumbled to herself.

She stared at the broken lead for a second, then set the pencil down carefully so she wouldn't break something else by accident. Around her, students all aspiring to be marksmen, duelists, healers, and a few in between. Most of them were talking about last night as Cole's monotone voice drowned beneath whispers.

"B-tier."

"No way."

"I heard it was planted."

They spoke the way people talked about celebrities and this was just the latest scoop. As if nothing has died a few classrooms down. Cole took control of the class, erasing the board and walking around the room to begin his next lesson. He wasn't the <u>Saint</u>, the Premier, nor an administrator. Just Head Field Instructor Cole, fifteen years at the Academy, long enough to treat survival like doctrine and doctrine like faith.

He wrote a word across the board in a clean, sharp line.

RESONANCE

Then, beneath it:

APPLICATION

He turned to face the room.

"Resonance is not philosophy," he declared. "<u>Resonance</u> is force trained through discipline. <u>Mana</u> becomes intent, <u>intent</u> outputs resonance, the <u>resonance residue</u> is what is left."

A few students nodded like he'd just said something holy. He lifted the chalk again and drew three simple columns.

DETECTION

ASSESSMENT

RESPONSE

"You detect," he began, tapping the first column. "You assess. You respond."

His chalk tapped the second, then the third.

"Assessment determines classification. Classification determines permitted response."

He tapped the third, harder.

"Your personal feelings are not a factor."

Stella felt her stomach tighten.

"A passive spirit is not the same thing as a harmless spirit," he claimed. "A spirit that appears inactive may be bait. A spirit that appears human may be wearing a human shape to make you hesitate."

His eyes swept the room as he paced back and forth.

"Hesitation gets people killed."

The room stayed quiet, actually attentive for the first time today.

He moved to the board again and wrote a second word beneath Response.

EXTERMINATION

Chalk dust drifted down. The word looked too heavy for chalk.

"Extermination is not cruelty," he stated without hesitation. "It is prevention. It is the reason your cities still stand."

Stella's grip on her notebook tightened without her noticing.

"The Great Resonance War taught us what happens when we treat spirits as misunderstood."

Her heart thudded hard enough for her to assume it could be heard nearby.

"Your duty is not to understand spirits," he explained. "Your duty is to end threats. It doesn't matter how cleanly you do it, but how quick. Otherwise, the civilian body count becomes a statistic you have to explain."

Because that was the problem, right? Fear decides what gets labeled a threat.

Stella looked down the row. Yumi sat one seat away, leaning back like she belonged in every room she'd ever entered. Her orange hair fell forward, half shadowing her green eyes. Her posture said relaxed, but Stella had seen her last night. She knew how quickly relaxed could become lethal.

Cole turned back to the board and began writing classifications.

D-tier.

C-tier.

B-tier.

A-tier.

S-tier.

No tier.

Each one with a corresponding response.

Stella's pulse climbed. She'd spent half the night awake with the words in her mouth, rephrasing until they didn't sound like something the administration would punish her for asking.

Idiot, don't do it.

She lifted her hand slightly, just to test herself. Yumi subtly shifted towards her as a response. Yumi leaned closer to Stella, just enough for her voice to reach Stella and no one else.

"Stella," she murmured.

Stella's hand froze halfway.

Yumi didn't look at her when she said it. Her eyes stayed forward, fixed on the board like she was still listening.

"Please don't," she whispered with intense, protective eyes.

It wasn't mocking or fake-sweet like what she did on the first day. She kept her voice quiet and urgent as if she was trying to stop a friend from stepping into a trap.

Stella almost lowered her hand.

Almost.

Last night had already been a trial and she'd failed something inside herself by staying quiet. She wouldn't do it again.

Her gaze dropped to her notebook.

EXTERMINATION.

And behind it, the image of that spirit in the classroom. Aggressive? Yes. Wrong place for it to be? Sure. Even then, it was just existing before Yumi ended it like she was swatting a fly.

Stella fully extended her hand. The motion was small, but it felt like slamming a door open in a storm.

Cole paused mid-sentence. He turned, eyes narrowing slightly. His expression was emotionless.

"Yes," he called out. "Devigne."

The room shifted.

You could feel it when attention turned on you. It felt like heat on bare skin. Stella slowly lowered her hand and kept her voice steady.

"Sir," she began, hating how careful she sounded. "You said extermination is prevention. That hesitation kills."

He nodded once, like this was acceptable so far and he had no reason to think otherwise. She took a breath.

"Saint Laurena stated publicly that action isn't justified if the spirit remains passive."

The moment the name left her mouth, the air changed. Everyone had an opinion about Saint Laurena.

A few students exchanged glances. A quiet snicker came from somewhere behind Stella. Yumi's head dipped slightly as she was looking at Stella, but began to look down at her desk.

"Please," the gesture implied. "Why would you do this to yourself?"

Stella didn't look at her.

"If a spirit is not attacking," she continued, "if it's not escalating, shouldn't we attempt common ground before force?"

A pause cut the air like a sword in still wind. Her own words echoed back at her and sounded ridiculous. Stella fully believed in what she said, but she could already hear how it would be filed.

Cole didn't react the way she expected. He stared at her for a long moment, like he was deciding whether to treat her like a student or a hazard. He slowly walked closer to the board to put the chalk down.

"Thank you," he asserted flatly.

The room went still.

"You're not wrong to be confused," he continued as he walked towards the class. "You are also not wrong to listen when a Saint speaks. Saints carry history."

He paced once, slow and controlled.

"But Saint Laurena does not teach this classroom. She speaks from Parliament inside of political buildings. Those ideals can afford distance."

Stella's stomach dropped. She knew where this was going. The defense that sounded reasonable until you noticed what it excused.

"We teach what happens when you are out of time," Cole preached, turning away to pace the floor. "When you don't get a second chance and civilians die in the streets while you're still trying to 'understand' the spirit."

He turned back to the students, eyes sweeping the class.

"There are soldiers and alumni students who visit this academy and have watched friends get hollowed out by something that looked passive right up until it wasn't."

A few students nodded harder now, like he'd finally spoken the truth. Heat crawled up Stella's neck.

"I'm not saying we never use force," Stella pleaded. "I'm saying—if it isn't attacking—then killing it shouldn't be the first answer."

If it's a boy shaped like a snail.

She didn't say that part. In this room, compassion sounded like stupidity.

Cole put his hands on his desk, fixing his eyes directly at Stella. His lips began to move as he stopped her gently.

"Devigne," he answered, his tone softening just enough to sting. "The reason your question is dangerous is because it assumes you will always know what you're looking at."

She went cold.

"You won't. You will see something that looks afraid and you will hesitate. It will kill someone who trusted you to act."

His voice grew even more quiet, but had strong resolve, "And you will spend the rest of your life wishing you had been cruel sooner."

Stella's throat tightened.

Somewhere behind her, someone whispered, "that's cute," followed by a soft laugh.

She didn't look back.

"Saint Laurena herself said—"

"Laurena is a Saint. She can afford to speak of hesitation. She has people whose entire job is to survive long enough to make that kind of voice possible."

Stella's fingers curled into her palm. She couldn't fathom how someone can feel this way.

"So your answer," she said standing up, voice shaking now despite everything she'd tried, "is that we kill first—because we're afraid of being wrong?"

A murmur rolled through the room. Cole stared at her like she'd finally shown her real face.

"No. We kill first because we've been taught what happens when we don't."

He turned back to the board.

"Sit down, Devigne."

It wasn't cruel, but a decisive choice he made about the topic and would now close.

Stella slowly sat down and faced forward. She saw Yumi staring at her and as she met her gaze, Yumi gave her a soft nod.

Cole pressed the chalk against the chalkboard and lectured as pages turned and students adjusted their chairs, even slightly dragging them into place. Stella opened her notebook.

"If I'm going to be here," she wrote, "I can't be invisible."

"And if I'm going to be removed, I need to understand why."

Chapter 7: Donuts

Cedric, Kai, Yumi, and Stella walked out of Cole's class. They didn't say anything as they approached the staircase. Yumi twisted her torso to crack her back.

"Man," she commented, rolling her shoulders. "I really needed that."

Kai laughed softly as he adjusted the strap of his bag. "You always say that."

"That's because it's always true," Yumi replied easily.

Cedric glanced back at Stella briefly, checking her pace without slowing down. "Everyone good?" he asked.

Stella nodded as she tried to give a reassuring face. "Yeah."

Yumi tried to lighten the mood with her usual complaint, "Instructor Cole's class always makes me want to fall asleep, I need some sugar."

They stopped near the vending machines tucked into the corner of the hall. A few students were already gathered there, coins clinking through the slot and conversations overlapping. Cedric stepped toward vending machines, glanced at the selection, and frowned slightly.

"I'll grab something downstairs," he informed the group as he made his way towards the staircase. "Cafeteria's probably closing."

Yumi perked up instantly. "Oh! Get me something sweet. Or salty. Or both. Actually, surprise me."

"You just ate lunch," Kai shot back.

Yumi scoffed. "That was hours ago."

"It was fourth period."

"Exactly," she answered, "that's the point."

Kai shook his head, smiling despite himself. "You're outrageous."

"Don't act like you aren't hungry now too," Yumi shot back. "I saw your face when I said sweet."

Kai opened his mouth to respond, but couldn't find the words to rationalize an excuse as his eyes grew big.

"...Okay, maybe a little."

Stella couldn't stop her stomach from growling. It was barely audible but it might as well have echoed since Yumi heard it loud and clear.

Yumi's head instantly snapped toward Stella. "Oh?" she remarked, grinning. "Are you hungry too, Stella?"

"I forgot to eat," Stella responded with a straight tone.

Yumi laughed with amusement in her eyes. "That's a yes."

Cedric returned then, holding a small paper bag and a cup. He handed the drink to Kai before setting the bag down on the edge of the vending machine.

"The cafeteria was about to close," he enlightened the trio. "So, donuts."

He opened the bag. The sweet smell of the deep fried breading and sugary frosting made its rounds through the hallway. Yumi leaned over to look inside. "You're forgiven, this will do," as she picked up a maple donut.

Kai reached in and took one. "You always get food," he interjected. "Do you just... plan for this?"

Cedric shrugged. "People get happy when they're fed."

Yumi snorted in laughter. "They do say the way to one's heart is their stomach."

Stella hesitated, then reached for the bag.

Cedric noticed. "Go ahead," he assured softly.

She took one carefully. "Thank you."

The donut was still hot. The warmth made it much more appealing than the packaged ones in the machine. She took a bite before she could think too hard about it.

Yumi watched her with open curiosity. "So," she said with a smile, "important question."

Stella looked up as she chewed the glazed treat. "Hm?"

"What's your favorite donut flavor?" Yumi asked. "This is critical information."

Stella glanced down at the donut in her hand. She hadn't thought about it in years.

"...I don't know," she said slowly. "Maybe... plain? Or glazed."

Yumi made a face. "That's not an answer, hmph."

Kai laughed as his chuckle filled the hall. "Glazed is respectable."

Cedric nodded while grinning. "Reliable choice."

Cedric straightened immediately. "Alright," he began while tossing the empty bag. "Let's move before we're late."

Yumi tossed the rest of her donut into her mouth and brushed her hands together. "Back to reality."

They started walking again, merging into the stream of students also headed to the staircase. They stayed in unison as they approached Miss Kim's class.

Cedric Pentaguarde, Fourth Year

Student Council President

The Academy

Chapter 8: Compliance

One Month Earlier

The academy's administration boardroom remained dim despite the afternoon hour. Tall windows lined the far wall, curtains drawn just enough to dull the sunlight into narrow bands that stretched across the length of the table. Files sat in careful stacks, grouped by color and seal. The national flag stood in the corner, unmoving, beside a bookshelf that carried bound volumes of Union history arranged by era rather than topic.

Saint Laurena stood at the far end of the room, facing the academy's Dean and his assistant. She had entered alone, leaving her <u>High Vanguard</u> and <u>High Priestess</u> outside the door. Her posture was upright, hands loosely folded behind her back, expression controlled but tight at the edges.

"For the last decade, this academy has stopped following its own rules."

No one responded immediately. The Dean remained seated, hands resting flat on the table. His assistant's eyes cut briefly to the files in front of him before returning to Laurena.

"That may have worked under the last Saint," Laurena continued, her voice level, "but not continue under my administration."

The Dean cleared his throat to cut the silence, choosing his words carefully.

"With respect, Saint Laurena," he pleaded, "the academy does represent the Harmony faction. Kai Claremont improves Yumi Lumiere's reliability in combat scenarios."

Laurena tilted her head slightly in annoyance, expecting this textbook answer from an administrator like him.

"You mean the boy who stands beside Yumi at all times."

She didn't wait for an answer as she pressed on.

"Please," Laurena stated. "He isn't Harmony."

She began to pace towards the table as she spoke.

"He exists to carry Yumi's ambition farther than she could alone."

Her gaze moved slowly from face to face.

"You have mistaken ambition for balance."

"You do not represent Harmony," Laurena continued. "You fold it into the Martial faction and call it equality."

The assistant replied, "then what would you have us do?"

The Saint slid a file that she was carrying close to her chest the whole time. The brown folder was slid across the table as the Dean looked at the header. The name was in bold, no doubt of who else it could have been.

Stella Devigne.

"This is Harmony,"

Neither administrator argued.

"A student who resolves passive spirit incidents without escalation," she concluded. "No spectacle or unnecessary losses happened, just outcome after outcome in silence."

She straightened.

"You sidelined her because peace does not photograph well in reports. The only thing that matters to this academy is combat."

The Dean was flustered, knowing that they were getting cornered.

"Saint... this girl has never trained in combat before, at least not under our curriculum."

Laurena met his eyes with strong conviction.

"Yes," she answered. "That is the point."

Tension grew thick in the air.

"You have allowed one faction to dominate this institution," Laurena asserted. "You will correct it."

She folded her hands behind her back and turned around, walking toward the door.

"The <u>Harmony Party</u> has decided. Stella Devigne will be appointed Student Council Vice President."

The Dean inhaled to speak.

"No," Laurena said calmly, hand already gripping the handle of the door. "This is not a discussion. It is compliance towards equal representation within what should be the most respected academy in the Union."

Laurena concluded, "if you honor this *recommendation* from the chamber, this matter remains internal."

She paused.

"If you don't, I will bring it to Parliament, publicly. Institutional discrimination headlines will be read on every paper."

The threat settled as Laurena opened the door.

"...Immediately?" The Dean asked.

Laurena nodded. "Yes, immediately."

The door closed as she left the room. For a long moment, the only sound was the low hum of the lights. The Dean exhaled in defeat.

"Well," he murmured quietly. "We'll comply."

"Of course," the assistant agreed instantly.

The Dean tapped the file once as the idea came to his head. "She didn't specify duration."

"...Temporary Vice President," the Dean concluded, eyes on the file as he turned the first page. He read the name aloud.

"Stella Devigne."

Pens came out immediately. The draft was already written before Laurena even exited the building.

Subject: Devigne, Stella

Proposed Role: Vice President, Student Council (Temporary)

Appointment is granted on a **conditional and revocable basis**, subject to continuous performance review and behavioral compliance.

Due to the subject's **non-standard ideological alignment**, enhanced oversight will be enacted. Failure to meet review standards may result in immediate reassignment.

Signed by:

Date:

Chapter 9: Bloodline

Miss Kim was halfway through her lecture when multiple footsteps filled the hallway. The sound was steady and in unison, way too heavy to belong to students. A few students began to lean towards the door, trying to get as close to the door as possible.

The figures passed the classroom door as the class caught a glance of the people. Medals shined against the hallway lights as six soldiers wearing ceremonial military uniforms moved in formation. Two High Battle Mages walked at the front with their posture rigid, followed by High Priests and Priestesses at the rear. At the center was a man in a navy blue suit, a national pin fixed neatly to his chest. Beside him walked a young man who resembled his appearance. He was no more than twenty.

The Dean approached the group from a distance.

"Well," he said warmly, a touch too practiced, "if it isn't the heir to House Devigne. How was your morning, sir?"

"Productive," he replied calmly. "Thank you."

As they moved on, the hallway noise grew faint.

"Is it true his son doesn't have resonance or mana blessings, like the rest of House Devigne?"

"Doesn't matter. The heir's bloodline still carries weight."

"Any other family would've been corrected by now. This one never is. Figures."

Harmony wasn't welcomed here, bloodlines were.

"Still. Imagine being born into that and coming up empty. His son is lucky."

Stella looked back down at her desk.

"Oh right... I had a father once."

The memory surfaced before she could stop it. Stella was four, standing barefoot on the cool tile of the hallway in her mother's house. The lights were dim and the sound of nature came from the windows. Her father stood at the end of the hall, facing a door she wasn't allowed near.

"Daddy," she asked, tugging lightly at the back of his sleeve, "what's that room?"

He spoke without turning towards her as he was typing in the lock code.

"It's meant for adults, Stella," he said firmly, almost dismissive.

She thought about that. Adults did many things that children didn't, she was always excited to become part of that world.

She nodded once, then asked, "Can I go there when I'm an adult, Dad?"

He finally faced her direction, then looked down towards her. He squatted to her level and looked young Stella in the eyes.

"You're a good girl, Stella. Take care of your mother."

Then he walked past her, his steps steady as he moved down the hall. Stella stayed where she was, nodding her head at him even though he was already gone. She turned back, staring at the closed door. She never asked about that door ever again.

Miss Kim cleared her throat, and the classroom came back into focus as she returned to the front of the room without comment, picking up where she had left off. Stella returned to her seat and followed along with the lecture at first.

Her thoughts drifted. Her mother at home, the vault hidden behind the bookshelf, her mind refused to settle on any topic.

"Stella Devigne."

She blinked back to reality.

"Huh?"

A few heads turned as Stella was caught off guard.

"Please focus," Miss Kim stated. "Yes or no."

Stella straightened while glaring at the board. "I'm sorry. Could you ask it again?"

Miss Kim sighed and studied her for a moment, then repeated the question with the same tone.

"Can a duelist defeat a mage if the mage is using damage reflect?"

"Yes, as long as the resonant damage output outweighs the shield and mana regeneration."

"Right. Good job, Stella. Please pay attention next time."

Miss Kim turned back to the board and continued without pause. The lecture resumed as normal until the monotone lesson was interrupted.

"Attention, students," the intercom announced abruptly. "By order of the Academy and external oversight, the annual engagement evaluation will commence immediately following sixth period. Attendance is mandatory."

Mandatory meant no delays and no room to fall behind, academically or otherwise.

The room digested the announcement, then they began to shift in pieces. A few students checked their schedules, as if confirming something they already suspected. Someone let out a quiet breath, followed by a complaint from another.

"Already?"

"They're moving it up," someone muttered. "That's not normal."

Miss Kim paused only long enough to tap the wood of her desk.

"You heard the announcement," she said without question. "Pack what you need."

Stella closed her notebook and began to pack her supplies. Around her, bags were lifted, straps adjusted, and conversations resumed.

The dismissal bell rang as the students filed into the hallway in uneven clusters, making their way to the staircase. Teachers lingered at their doors, watching without comment as the flow passed by. In the courtyard, uniformed personnel were already visible, making sure the event was organized and secure. Stella joined the stream without thinking, matching pace as the hallway narrowed and pressure built toward the exits.

"That's right!" Stella reminded herself as her body moved in the packed hallway. "My staff is in my locker."

Student council members were authorized to carry arms on campus.

Chapter 10: Annual Combat Tournament

Stella stopped by her locker and retrieved her staff before heading outside. It felt light and familiar in her hand as she wrapped her fingers around the handle. The courtyard was already filled with students. She spotted the rest of the council standing near the front rows.

Cedric stood in the center, sword resting at his hip in Pentaguarde red. Yumi lounged beside him, hands in the air as she stretched and yawned, her sniper balanced loosely in one hand. A few steps away, Kai whispered under his breath, buffing sigils threading through his fingers like a practiced ritual.

"Hey guys," Stella greeted as she joined them.

"Good morning, Stella," Cedric replied, smiling.

"Hey Stel," Yumi replied while yawning. "You ready for your first tournament run with the council?"

"You'll do just fine," Kai stated with a grin.

"I'll—"

A sharp tap on the microphone cut her off.

"Good morning, students," the Dean announced. "Thank you for participating in today's tournament."

His eyes began to pan the courtyard left to right.

"House Devigne will be observing the event. Do not let that distract you."

Whispers began to spread throughout the courtyard.

"Six teams have been selected this year to compete."

The semifinals passed in a blur of noise and motion. Four teams entered the arena with only two advancing.

The council's match unfolded fast and ugly. Snow covered sightlines as orders came clipped and automatic. Stella rotated on cue, deployed shields on instinct, and was eliminated early when the opposing team baited her barrier and punished the opening. Her name vanished from the nameboard before she finished falling.

"BLUE TEAM CONTESTANT ELIMINATED."

Stella walked out the arena, taking off her helmet to get some fresh air. As she left the back entrance, she saw a blue figure, covered in red, dried liquid being carried by three soldiers. She squinted her eyes as she walked toward the area. Her view was blocked by a green coat over a royal blue uniform.

"This area is off limits, medical personnel only." The soldier was carrying a first aid kit. "Please go back to the lobby."

She walked toward the arena. When she turned around, the people at a distance were no longer in sight.

"BLUE TEAM VICTORY."

The rest of the council secured the win. Stella's name appeared on the board again as staff prepared to arena for the finals. Stella made her way to the cafeteria.

Chapter 11: Tournament Lunch

The cafeteria buzzed long before the council reached the doors. Trays scraped against counters. Voices overlapped in uneven waves. The smell of food hung thick in the air, steak, lobster, roasted potatoes, chocolate, all rich enough that students slowed just to take it in. Brochures lined the walls beneath the academy crest, neatly printed menus titled,

ANNUAL TOURNAMENT LUNCH

The council stood partway through the line, boxed in by students comparing options and craning their necks toward the serving counter.

"I'm so excited for this lunch," Yumi announced, already grinning. "I heard they're serving steak for the event."

She snatched a handful of brochures from the wall and handed them out without breaking stride. "Alright! What do you guys plan on getting?"

Cedric glanced down at the menu, already decided. "Southwest salad with grilled chicken," he responded. "I'd like to stay light for the finals."

Yumi groaned. "That's the least exciting answer possible."

"It gets the job done."

"I'll probably try the *'queen-noah'* with grilled salmon," Kai said after a moment. "I've never had it before."

Yumi stopped walking. "You mean quinoa? We had that at the taco place last month."

"Oh." Kai confused, thinking back. "So that's how you say it. It feels like tiny fishballs."

"That is not what fishballs feel like," Yumi commented.

Kai shrugged, unapologetic.

Yumi turned to the last brochure holder. "What about you, Stella?"

Stella stood still, staring at the blueberry cobbler, covered in red jelly. She immediately shook her head.

"I'm sorry, can you ask again?"

"The menu Stel, what will you get?"

"Honestly? The garlic noodles sound really good, I guess..." she replied softly, barely looking at the brochure.

Yumi's eyes lit up. "Excellent taste. You should get it with that and the fried chicken."

"That's not how menus work," Kai commented.

"That's how celebrations work," Yumi argued, smiling.

The line crawled forward. Students hesitated at the counter, changing their minds at the last second. Laughter broke out from someone reading the menu incorrectly. Someone cheered when their tray was handed over. They found an open table near the windows and set their trays down in staggered clacks, the noise of the room swelling around them. For a few seconds, no one spoke. Then Yumi took a bite, froze, and stared at her plate.

"...Okay," she began with a mouth full of food. "No. This is actually amazing. I wonder if they'll allow seconds."

Cedric chuckled, chewed, then shifted the topic.

"Since this is our last year, what do you guys want to do after? I've got mine planned out, I'm just curious where everyone's headed."

Yumi swallowed. "I want recommendations to join the Union Army as an officer," she informed the group. "It'd be cool to lead a squad early. What about you guys?"

"I'm joining the Union Army too," Kai said with a smile. "Yumi and I are planning to request the same three bases so we can stay nearby."

Yumi reached over and grabbed Kai's chocolate chip cookie. "Well, that's if they allow it," she shot back. "But tournament winners get station priority. I can't see it *not* happening."

Stella twirled her noodles, thinking.

"I'd like to keep saving spirits without violence," she answered. "The same way I've been doing the past three years, before joining the council."

Cedric replied without hesitation. "That's consistent, I respect that."

"-or dangerously ambitious," Yumi added, already chewing. "You're leaving it to chance."

Kai nodded. "I get it. I want to protect Yumi the same way you want to protect spirits."

Yumi raised a brow. "So you're calling me a spirit now?"

"That's not what I meant."

"What I *do* know," Yumi said grinning while eyeing the table, "is that you guys haven't eaten your cookies. Stella? Cedric?"

Laughter carried for a moment, then the bell rang.

Chapter 12: End of the Bracket

The council approached the arena for the final time that day. Having just finished lunch, the team felt energized as they stepped into their assigned body tubes one by one. The arena sealed shut, cutting off the cheers of the audience.

"The last match of the tournament, folks!" the announcer said in a hyped-up voice. "Can Team Green perform an upset and defeat Team Blue in the Forest Arena?"

"Gates opening in five-"

The council slid down the hill in practiced synergy.

"Four."

Cedric gave Stella a thumbs-up.

"Three."

Yumi glanced down at her scope, testing her vision.

"Two."

Stella nodded back toward Cedric.

"One."

The gates opened.

The field was different from the last two, much quieter and less chaotic. The arena was a jungle, thick with trees, tall bushes, and hanging branches. There was no storm this time. The air was clear and still.

Yumi climbed the tallest tree nearby, settling into its upper branches. Kai stayed on ground level, slightly ahead of her, hidden in a bush. Cedric and Stella sprinted straight for the dome without hesitation, beating the opposing team to the center.

Three lanes fed into the middle of the field. Kai poured his mana into Stella, charging her reserves just long enough for her to deploy two barriers. The enemy team was forced to take the right lane.

Cedric positioned himself beside a bush between the middle and right lanes just as a smoke screen dropped, swallowing visibility across the field.

"An illusion mage," Stella realized.

Cedric moved closer to the edge of the smoke, the bush at its tip. His hand rested on his hilt.

Footsteps, approaching close.

Cedric lowered his stance and narrowed his eyes. A green silhouette emerged through the smoke, a rifleman clearing corners. He moved with discipline, weapon up, scanning the brush. Behind him followed a swordsman, heavy-set and tank-like in build. Cedric hugged the tree line, staying concealed.

Kai's fatigue set in. The middle barrier flickered, then collapsed, opening a narrow gap. Still, three enemy contestants were now accounted for in the right lane.

As the rifleman cleared the corner, the swordsman walked straight past Cedric's hiding spot. Cedric didn't hesitate. He drew his blade and struck horizontally, aiming for the jaw.

Slash.

The swordsman dropped instantly.

"GREEN TEAM CONTESTANT ELIMINATED."

Gunfire tore through the brush. Stella reacted immediately, forming a barrier around the bush as Cedric pulled back. Someone slipped through the cover as the gunman finished reloading. He aimed at Cedric, but Yumi shot his hand, forcing the rifle to drop. Cedric turned around to see the hidden attacker, ending the threat immediately.

"GREEN TEAM CONTESTANT ELIMINATED."

The gunman, now one-handed, picked up his fallen ally's sword and rushed for the back of Cedric's head. Stella pushed off without thinking, her legs barely keeping up. Her mana spent on shield upkeep.

BOOM.

She slammed into the marksman shoulder-first. Both of them crashed to the ground.

Cedric turned just in time to understand what she'd done to keep him in the match.

"GREEN TEAM CONTESTANT ELIMINATED."

"BLUE TEAM CONTESTANT ELIMINATED."

A flashbang detonated. When vision returned, the smoke was gone and all illusions had collapsed.

The final Green Team contestant, a mage, charged Cedric with a sword. It was futile. His resonance was never meant for close combat.

"GREEN TEAM WIPEOUT. BLUE TEAM VICTORY."

The awards were announced shortly after. Cedric was named Leader of the Series. Stella received Clutch Play of the Series from the finals. Yumi earned MVP of the Series.

Yumi Lumiere, Fourth Year

4x Tournament Contestant, 2x Tournament MVP

Student Council Treasurer

The Academy

Chapter 13: Silence in the Records

Stella exited sixth period, her final class of the day. Her council-privilege suspension had ended that morning. Tomorrow was her position review. The review would close doors that still gave Stella answers.

"I need to understand why that aggressive spirit was there last month," she thought to herself as her feet paced quickly. "If it passed Overwatch, there has to be a reason."

She turned down the main hall and nearly collided with Yumi.

"Hey, Stel!" Yumi greeted brightly, eyes closed with a wide grin. "You wanna come with me and Kai for tacos? They said they'll give me a free meal if I can eat ten fire tacos in ten minutes!"

Stella laughed, reciprocating a grin of her own. "You think you can do it?"

"No," Yumi answered immediately, already chuckling. "That's why it'll be exciting. You should come!"

"I appreciate the invite," Stella gently assured. "But I actually need to stop by the library first."

"No worries! Text me if you change your mind, okay?"

"It's a promise. Make sure to drink water!"

"We'll see! I can't drink milk apparently!" Yumi called back, already running toward Kai.

Stella watched them go as she stood still and waved them goodbye. She really did intend to meet them afterward. The smile faded as she turned toward the library.

LIBRARY

The doors slid open without resistance. Dusty shelves stretched across the interior, students hunched over tables, a handful of active-duty soldiers conducting quiet research near the back.

Stella slowed as she reached the inner corridor.

RESTRICTED ARCHIVES - STAFF AND COUNCIL ONLY

For a brief moment, habit made her hesitate. She scanned her badge as the locks disengaged, allowing her to step past the security control gate. Inside, shelves of doctrine lined the room. Martial versus Harmony, battlefield formations, procedural revisions spanning centuries of history leading to this moment. Cabinets of sealed records traced the foundations of the Union itself, the Pentaguarde and Devigne families threaded through its rise and fractures.

Stella moved straight to a terminal.

"There it is," she murmured.

ACADEMY PROCEDURES

She skimmed through the folder and read a singular file carefully.

<u>Academy Pylon Procedures</u>

Three-layer pylon array. Directional resonance scanning. Any D-tier classification or higher notifies Overwatch.

Nearest military support: thirty minutes.

Faculty priority: student evacuation.

Student Council: buffer and delay.

Military vanguard personnel: attack and secure the spirit.

Her gaze stopped.

Military mage personnel: contain and hold the spirit.

Stella stared at the line longer than the rest.

"What if there aren't any military mages stationed here?" she wondered. "I've never seen one on campus. And this environment doesn't exactly invite mages."

She exhaled and backed out of the file. "If procedures didn't explain it, history might."

She opened older archives.

"There," she said quietly with resolve.

ACADEMY DOCTRINE.

Academy Doctrine Revision - Strategic Forecast Addendum

Date: 100 years prior

Author: General Cousins

"Comparative analysis of Imperial and Union combat readiness indicates a fundamental doctrinal mismatch."

"The Imperial Army, under the Pentaguarde dynastic command, trains for sustained, high-casualty engagement with extreme combat discipline."

"Harmony-aligned methodologies have demonstrated effectiveness in localized containment and post-catastrophe stabilization."

"However, <u>Harmony doctrine</u> does not scale under projected conditions of prolonged multi-front invasion."

"In a total-war scenario, delayed response and discretionary engagement significantly increase civilian attrition."

Stella leaned back slowly and fixed her eyes on the final line.

"For long-term survival, <u>martial doctrine</u> must be prioritized, effectively reducing harmony doctrine."

"This wasn't a recent decision," she murmured. "It was a future decided long before I was born."

Still, something didn't fit. Stella pulled up archived Overwatch summaries and began cross-referencing dates. Older reports flagged more spirit activities than the ones in the present day. There was no catastrophe, reform, or major recalibration in modern history for a sudden drop in spirit activity.

"Nothing changed," Stella whispered. "So why did the reports stop matching reality?"

Her eyes returned to the terminal.

"Unless..." she concluded. "Unless they never fell... unless it was disabled."

Stella closed the file and immediately forgot why she had stood up.

"If the pylons hadn't failed, then someone had made sure they never sounded."

The thought settled slowly in her chest. Hours passed without her noticing. Midnight arrived quietly. At some point, Stella's head lowered onto the desk. Four books lay open around her and she fell asleep before she realized it.

Chapter 14: Red Alert

The door to the restricted archives slammed open.

"Stella!"

The voice cut through the quiet and jolted her awake. Stella stirred with her cheek pressed against the wooden table, inked pages spread beneath her hands. Her staff rested where she had left it, close enough that her fingers brushed the shaft as she lifted her head.

"Stella, wake up."

Her eyes opened slowly. Purple hair fell across her face as she tried to focus. "Yumi...?"

Yumi did not answer, eyes filled with fear. She crossed the room in two steps, grabbed Stella's wrist, and pulled.

"We have to go. Now."

Stella stood before the urgency fully settled in. Her hand closed around her staff out of habit as Yumi dragged her into the corridor and broke into a run. They reached the courtyard just as movement swelled around them.

Faculty voices overlapped as doors opened and shut. Boots scraped across stone. Students clustered in uneven groups, some moving, others frozen where they stood. The alarm cut through the noise a moment later.

Red Alert.

The words echoed through the space as Stella and Yumi reached Kai and Cedric, already facing the administrators.

"Sir," Kai began nervously, his brow furrowed. "Do we have authority to defend the academy without instructor presence?"

The Dean responded without hesitation. "You are fully authorized. Instructors will lead the evacuation. You will protect the retreat."

He stepped forward into the center of the courtyard and raised his voice.

"Attention."

The noise thinned as people turned towards him.

"We are on Red Alert. Faculty will evacuate all students through the east corridor. The student council will sweep the buildings for anyone left behind, then return here to support the retreat and act as a buffer."

He paused briefly, long enough for the weight of the order to settle.

"Active military will intercept the threat."

He turned away as he abruptly finished his speech. Several uniformed soldiers stood nearby, hands already resting on their weapons.

"Sir," Kai said, stopping him. "We don't have any military mages on site."

The Dean slowed but did not look back.

"You will have to make do with what you have."

He continued toward the east wing without another word. The soldiers shifted toward the west corridor, weapons coming up with practiced efficiency. Cedric turned to the council.

"Stella, north halls. Yumi, east. Kai, south. I'll take the west," he commanded. "Escort anyone you find to the east gate. We regroup at the covered walkway."

They separated without argument. Stella sprinted through campus, her hair streaming behind her as the wind tore past. The now abandoned north wing was quiet.

Stella moved quickly, entering the first hall and checking each room in sequence. Classroom doors stood open where students had fled. Papers lay scattered across desks and floors. A chair had been knocked onto its side near a window, sunlight spilling across it as if the room had been abandoned mid-lesson.

She called out once and was met with silence. The stairwell echoed as she moved to the next building. It was the same there. Empty corridors and locked storage rooms gave no response. Only the sound of her own footsteps following her down the hall.

By the time she reached the third building, the air felt heavier. Her grip tightened around the staff as she cleared the ground floor.

That was when she finally heard a noise. Soft at first. She stood still, then heard the faint sound again.

Crying.

Stella turned toward the stairwell and climbed to the second floor, taking the steps two at a time. The sound led her to a classroom near the end of the hall.

"Hello?" she called, keeping her voice low. "Is anyone here?"

There was no reply. She pushed the class door open. A first-year was crouched in the corner between the teacher's desk and the windows, arms wrapped tight around herself. Her shoulders shook as she tried to stay quiet. Stella stopped just inside the doorway. She set her staff carefully against the desk and stepped forward with her hands open.

"It's okay," Stella whispered gently. "I'm here."

The student looked up. Her eyes were red and unfocused. She did not move. Stella closed the distance slowly and reached out. Gunfire cracked through the air. The sound made Stella flinch. The student folded inward, pressing her face into her sweater with a silent scream as the rifle emptied somewhere beyond the building.

"It isn't safe here," Stella informed the girl, voice lowered. "We need to leave. I'll take you to the evacuation."

She reached out again. This time, the student's hand met hers. It was stiff and unresponsive. Stella tightened her grip.

"Stay close."

The student nodded and stood, clinging to Stella's sleeve as they moved back into the hall.

They reached the east gate minutes later. Faculty were already organizing lines, guiding students through in controlled groups. Stella led the first-year forward and waited until an instructor took her by the shoulder.

"North halls are clear," Stella announced. "One student recovered."

The instructor nodded. "Understood. Take the rear until the others arrive."

Stella stayed long enough to help steady the line. Moments later, Yumi, Kai, and Cedric emerged from the opposite side of the courtyard. Seven students in total were brought through.

The Dean addressed them as they regrouped. "Council, to the courtyard. Support the soldiers."

Chapter 15: Stay With Me, Kai

They moved immediately. Stella saw the bodies. Three soldiers lay where they had fallen. Two crushed near the edge of the courtyard. Another was slumped against the wall of a nearby building.

Only two remained standing.

Ahead of them, the spirit wrenched a tree from the ground. The academy grounds, once orderly and familiar, now resembled a graveyard. The two remaining soldiers fired resonant rounds until their weapons clipped empty. The spirit barely recoiled before bringing the tree down on the soldiers. No barrier intercepted the blow, reducing the duo to nothing as their bodies erased into the ground.

The council arrived moments later, skidding to a halt near the covered walkway.

"Formation!" Cedric ordered his team.

They split without hesitation. Stella veered left toward the end of the covered walkway. Cedric pressed forward to position himself closest to the spirit. Yumi and Kai broke right, Yumi just a few steps ahead as she sprinted toward a tree and Kai followed as fast as he could.

The spirit hurled the tree towards the building. The impact collapsed the structure. Stone and metal sheared free, launching outward. Yumi instinctively slid beneath the falling debris, her feet skimming the grass as she reached her position. She reloaded her sniper in one fluid motion.

"Kai," she commanded, voice firm, "charge the bullets as they exit the chamber."

The wind roared past Yumi's ears as she fired. The shot ricocheted harmlessly off the spirit's core.

"I need charges now," Yumi snapped, already turning. "There's no penetra—"

Yumi finished turning her head with her eyes magnified. A familiar silhouette lay crushed beneath the slab, orange hair matted dark with blood.

The debris she ducked beneath had filled her vision. Beneath it, red spread across the grass toward her, stopping at the soles of her boots.

Blood from someone who should be alive.

Stella and Cedric had just settled in position when the scream tore through the courtyard. The horror from the sound was just enough for them to assume the worst. Their eyes confirmed the unthinkable.

Yumi had one hand on the slab pinning her friend. Her other hand hung useless as her rifle slipped from her grip. Blue liquid streamed from her chin, mixing with the red soaked on the ground.

Stella staggered backward. Her staff began to feel impossibly heavy.

"No... this wasn't supposed to happen," Stella thought to herself.

Her feet refused to move.

The spirit began to advance towards their position.

"Formation!" Cedric called again, but his command reached deaf ears.

Yumi seized two exposed metal beams torn free from the building. Her top teeth cut into her lip until blood began to leak. The beams bit into her palms as she clinched them hard and sprinted towards the spirit.

Yumi was not a duelist, but she moved like someone who needed to feel death with her own hands.

Cedric ran beside her, following her pace, positioning himself between her and the spirit.

"Stand down. Regroup. Now," Cedric ordered.

"Move," Yumi said, her voice fractured, raw with rage. "Unless you want to die with it."

She vaulted past a fallen boulder, using the motion to drive her heel into Cedric's chest, and sent him crashing to the ground.

The spirit swung wide. Yumi leaped over the stone arm and came down hard, driving the beams toward its core. Without technique or sword discipline, the metal scraped uselessly across hardened resonance. She screamed out as she threw a flurry of strikes, committing fully to each one.

She planted her feet for a thrust.

The spirit's arm met her without resistance. Her body was struck hard.

The collision sent Yumi flying into the building. The lifeless body of the orange-haired girl slowly slid down the wall, leaving red in its wake. Blood painted the walls which her body indented.

Stella stood motionless as the dust settled around her. Not a single mage was present in the courtyard, only lifeless vanguard soldiers. The spirit approached unopposed.

Chapter 16: Before Tomorrow

The spirit shook the ground with each step as it approached the last remaining survivors. Stella stood petrified, eyes fixed on where Yumi had fallen. The body lay still, half-shadowed by debris, orange hair darkened where blood had soaked into the grass. The courtyard felt widened by the scene.

Cedric ran to her, sword still sheathed. He grabbed her by the hand and began to run.

"Stella. Move."

Her feet stumbled as he dragged her into the open field of the courtyard, farther away from the wreckage and bodies. The spirit slowly turned towards them.

"Stella," Cedric muttered as his breath grew tight. "I need you to use mana drainage on the spirit."

She shook her head before the words even formed. "It's too powerful," she replied, voice breaking, "I can't stop it."

"You don't need to stop it," he replied. "You just need to slow—"

"Then what?" she snapped, panic spilling over. "It killed the soldiers, Yumi, Kai—" her voice cracked. What do you think you and I can do?"

Cedric paused at the question, pondering the thought.

"I'm going to use Judgment Call," he informed Stella, voice low and steady.

She flinched in shock. "You'll kill yourself!"

He walked away as she finished her proclamation.

She grabbed his sleeve, "Cedric—"

He stopped but didn't turn. "If I don't," he hypothesized, "it will kill everyone."

Stella's grip loosened as Cedric walked away alone, closing distance to the spirit.

He dropped low and spoke the words, "Resonance activate, Judgment Call."

His eye ignited red. Resonance burned through his body, dark smoke spilling from his shoulders as his sword grew heavier and larger. Both hands locking around the hilt before surging forward.

Rocks burst outward with every hit as he struck the stone arms. The spirit answered with sweeping blows, but Stella forced herself to move, channeling mana drain into its limbs. Each strike slowed the spirit slightly, barely half a second. The drain made it possible for Cedric to dodge, cut, and reenter. The exchange remained violent and uneven. Cedric pushed forward through brute force, carving away at the spirit's arms, thinning them with each strike.

Stella began to notice before anything else.

"His shoulders are shaking... he's losing strength."

She raised instanced shields, one after another. Each barrier shattered instantly under the spirit's blows, but every break stole a fraction of momentum. Cedric was able to gain another half-second, another step for positioning.

Judgment Call took its toll as Cedric began to falter, his sword dipping. The spirit's arm crashed into him and sent him flying across the courtyard. He also smashed into the flagpole, skidding hard against the pavement.

Stella casted barriers toward him, desperate, but the spirit didn't slow as it approached the fallen swordsman. Cedric pushed himself upright, shaking, mouth dripping blood. He looked up at the spirit following in.

"At least you tried," he murmured, breath ragged. "You did more than enough."

The spirit loomed in front of him and lifted the fallen tree it had torn free earlier.

Stella ran, diving onto Cedric, as the spirit began to recoil its arm, preparing to smash the two survivors.

She wrapped her arms around him, burying her face against his chest as the impact rushed toward them. Tears soaked into his blazer, her hands trembling, heart collapsing inward.

First Kai, then Yumi. I can't lose you too. You're the last one I have left.

Stella screamed at the top of her lungs, "No!"

Resonance surged throughout her body, blinding and cold. Light skilled from her skin as everything locked into place. A sphere formed around her and Cedric, bright and blue at first, then hardening into crystallization. The crystal, now resembling a cocoon.

The tree struck as roots shattered. Bark exploded outward, but the crystal remained solid. The spirit slammed the remains against the cocoon again and again until the trunk splintered into branches. Some fist stones followed. Each blow sent shards flying, but the cocoon held. Slowly, the crystal began to fade.

The crystal thinned as resonance drained away. Cracks of transparency spread across its surface. The spirit pulled back its arm, gathering momentum for the final strike.

Bang.

A bullet tore through the spirit's chin. Stone fractured as its head snapped back.

"Reloading!" a voice shouted from a distance.

Four soldiers emerged across the courtyard, uniform royal blue with green stripes.

Capital Special Forces.

One of them sprinted to Cedric and Stella. He pressed two fingers to Stella's Neck.

"Good, still beating," he declared.

Cedric barely registered his presence. Stella was limp, completely drained.

"Now is not the time, Captain," a green-haired soldier called, already moving towards the spirit with twin blades drawn.

Facing his squad, the Captain nodded towards the soldier. "Charge!"

"Plats, Calder," the dualblader called.

The mage responded instantly, casting diagonal platforms formed in sequence as the one leapt forward, trusting each one to exist when her foot landed. She bounced between constructs and the spirit's arms, moving like a blade through collapsing space.

The spirit swung at the duelist as a sniper round struck its wrist mid-motion, collapsing the stone hand.

The dual-wielder spun, sliced through its eyes, landed, and launched again. Both swords drove into the core. The spirit collapsed as stone disintegrated into nothing.

"Thanks Calder, Theo," she said, sheathing her blades.

The four soldiers regrouped, scanning the courtyard as silence settled over the wreckage.

Chapter 17: Tag It, Kaede

The four soldiers approached Cedric and Stella, both still unconscious.

"Everyone," the Captain commanded, "scan the area and check for bodies."

All three moved immediately.

The mage knelt down beside two fallen soldiers, fingers pressed briefly against their necks. "Both these soldiers are dead. Time of death, roughly fifteen minutes ago."

"Confirmed. Tag it, Calder," the Captain replied.

"There's a deceased under debris," the sniper called out. "Body beyond recognition."

"That's unfortunate, Theo. Keep searching."

A moment later, the dualblader's voice cut through the courtyard. "Captain, there's a body here. No pulse, but resonance levels are through the roof."

"Tag and move, Kaede. We don't have time to lose."

The three regrouped near the Captain, who was already working to stabilize Cedric. He kept his movements steady as he patched his wounds.

"Report."

Kaede straightened herself. "Aside from the two injured students, seven total deaths are confirmed. One subject showed resonance activities inconsistent with the rest."

The captain did not hesitate. "Medics should be with the faculty by now. Let's get these two out first, then we retrieve the bodies of the fallen."

Cedric and Stella were carried carefully toward the gathering of evacuated students and staff.

The Dean stepped forward, his breath taken as he took in the scene. "My goodness... what is your name, soldier?"

"Ardan Reed. <u>Capital Special Operations Command</u>. Captain of the Fifth Rapid Response Detachment."

"And the other student council members?" the Dean asked. "The soldiers?"

Ardan lowered his gaze for a moment before answering. His voice remained calm, but soft. "They didn't make it."

A hush settled over the hill. What remained of the academy loomed behind them, cracked stone and twisted metal still warm from the collapse.

"That's unfortunate," the Dean replied quietly. "I hope their families can find peace."

Ardan looked back at him. "Where were the Overwatch workers? We should have been notified well before the spirit reached the school-grounds."

The Dean stiffened, "I assure you, Captain, I will get to the bottom of this. Please—tend to the bodies."

Ardan gave a half nod and told his soldiers to go back to the courtyard and wait for the recovery team to retrieve the bodies. Ardan briefly stayed in the evacuation site to talk to the medics before returning to his squad in the courtyard.

"Those two students will be joining us," he informed his lieutenants. "I've instructed the medics to have them transported to the capital headquarters once they're stable."

Kaede glanced at him with a slight tilt to her head. "Sir, are we holding them until things clear, or beginning training?"

"One of them is Pentaguarde," Ardan replied with confidence. "That much is clear."

He paused, rubbing his chin as the memory surfaced.

"The other produced a crystal. Crystalized resonance shouldn't be possible outside of one bloodline." He let the thought go without finishing it.

Ardan looked back at the courtyard. "Three, four, five..." he stopped. "Kaede."

"Yes, Captain?"

"You reported seven deceased. Where are the other two?"

Kaede frowned as she turned back to the marked remains. "That's weird. These are all soldiers. There were two students. Didn't the Dean refer to them as council members?"

Ardan's eyes narrowed. "We have to tell command. What were the exact resonance readings on the girl?"

Kaede answered him quietly. Ardan set his sights back to the courtyard.

Only the dark stains left behind in the grass marked where Yumi and Kai had been. No trace beyond what the ground had already absorbed.

The response arrived shortly after. Recovery teams moved in once the area was cleared, civilian coroners documenting what remained.

When the work was done, Ardan, Kaede, Theo, and Calder departed for city hall to report directly to the Premier.

Chapter 18: Good Job, Major

Ardan, Kaede, Theo, and Calder arrived at city hall shortly after sunrise. The heart of the capital was alive with noise and traffic as breaking news of the Academy's fall surfaced. Inside, honor guards paced the floors under direction of their squad leaders, moving with purpose as preparations quietly escalated. Union history lined the walls in long embroidered panels, every Premier and Saint name stitched in gold thread. Statues of the Pentaguarde and Devigne founders stood at the entrance, set forward-facing, equal in height and weight.

Behind the Pentaguarde statue sat the Martial Hall. The Premier's office is behind these doors. The group knew their way with no guidance like the back of their hand. The Premier sat behind his desk with a report already open, eyes fixed on the report even as his door opened.

"Thank you for your work, Fifth Rapid Response Detachment," he announced.

Ardan stepped forward, taking off his hat. "We're happy to be here, Premier Darius."

"Captain Reed," Darius called out firmly. "Stay. The rest of you may go."

Kaede, Calder, and Theo all looked at Ardan. He gave a quick grin and a nod of assurance. The three exited while closing the door behind them.

Darius stayed seated as he fixed his eyes on Ardan.

"My office already has the summaries," he informed Ardan. "So don't walk me through it."

"Yes, sir."

"The Academy fell during your response window."

"Sir, by the time Overwatch contacted us, the spirit was already active on campus. A-tier. We arrived in twenty minutes and—"

"Stop."

Ardan froze mid-breath, his words lingering at the tip of his tongue.

"Procedure allows thirty," Darius continued. "You arrived early."

"Yes, sir."

"And students still died."

Ardan opened his mouth to continue his summary. "The pylons did not respond. Faculty evacuation was already—"

"I am not asking why," Darius declared flatly. "I am telling you what the conclusion is."

Ardan closed his mouth, realizing the truth of the situation.

"There is no internal compromise listed in the Academy's reports," Darius stated. "You will not describe it that way."

"Yes, sir."

"The Academy is endorsed by this office," Darius continued. "If it failed due to corruption, that failure belongs here."

Now standing, he fixed his eyes on Ardan to find a reaction.

"Understood," Ardan replied, remaining still, looking down as he spoke.

"So," Darius started, both hands fixed on the table, "this becomes a matter of timing. You could have arrived faster. That is the version that stands."

Ardan's gaze remained on Darius's desk as he listened.

"But," Darius continued while his index finger traced the report, "your actions limited casualties. Faculty survived. Most students survived. Witnesses are already speaking favorably."

He turned back to face Ardan.

"That makes you the correct endpoint."

Darius closed the folder.

"I am promoting you," he said. "Major Ardan Reed. You are now in charge of the Capital Special Operations Command."

Ardan's eyes shot up at Darius's. "Sir?"

"The announcement is already written," Darius promptly informed him. "This is not a conversation."

Ardan swallowed, legs loosening as the words marinated. "My detachment is not prepared for reassignment."

"We will assign another captain."

"Then allow me time to prepare First Lieutenant Furukawa."

Darius looked at him for a long moment while his fingers tapped the file.

"Fine," he sharply muttered. "But understand this clearly."

He stepped away from his desk and approached Ardan.

"From now on, any questions about this incident will be answered by your name. If response time is criticized, it is yours. If decisions are questioned, they are yours."

Ardan solidified his noodle legs and met Darius's eyes. "Yes, sir."

Darius turned away and picked up a pen.

"You are dismissed, Major."

Ardan saluted, put his hat back on, and made his way to the door. He took a quick exhale as he gripped the handle, his officers waiting behind it for him.

The Academy, now in ruins, will remain investigated. The explanation to the media would hold to the public. The results will stay with Major Ardan no matter how the narrative shifts. Ardan exited the room and the four made their way back to the capital's military headquarters.

Glossary

Academy Pylon Procedures Procedures that explain the large-scale resonance sensors that detect hostile magical activity and automatically alert Overwatch.   *63*

Capital Special Operations Command (CSOC) The highest military command office in the capital, authorizing and coordinating elite special forces throughout the Union, led by a Major.   *81*

Harmony Doctrine A Union-aligned combat philosophy focused on containment, stabilization, and minimizing collateral damage rather than decisive elimination.   *63*

Harmony Party & Martial Party The Union's two ruling political parties, governing through doctrine, regulation, and centralized oversight rather than direct force.   *43*

High Priest(ess) An elite Union mage recognized for exceptional mastery of mana and resonance control, typically deployed in support, containment, or stabilization roles.   *40*

High Vanguard An elite Union combat operative recognized for exceptional battlefield performance using weaponry enhanced through mana and resonance.   *40*

Intent How the user shapes the mana into resonance.   *27*

Mana The raw energy available to work with magic.   *27*

Martial Doctrine A combat doctrine centered on rapid engagement, decisive force, and neutralizing threats as quickly as possible, prioritizing victory over containment. *63*

Premier The co-sovereign leader of the Union, representing the Martial Party, alongside the Saint of the Harmony Party. *2*

Pylon Large-scale resonance sensors used to detect and manage abnormal magical activity. *2*

Rapid Response Detachment A small, elite special forces unit designed for immediate response to threats involving the capital or national interest. The detachments containing Captain, Lieutenants, and Operators. *1*

Resonance The output of what mana delivers through the intent of the user. *27*

Resonance Residue The byproduct of resonance after the cast is complete. It is invisible to the natural eye, but can be scanned through technology or a resonance-scanning mage. *27*

Saint The co-sovereign leader of the Union, representing the Harmony Party, alongside the Premier of the Martial Party. *27*

The Academy The Union's prestigious national academy, best known for training elite military and political candidates. *1*

The Union The nation Stella lives in. Originally founded by House Pentaguarde and House Devigne of the Royal Court. *4*

Author's Note

Thank you so much for reading.

This project wouldn't have come together without Nikki "Serinnarie" Nguyen, who helped throughout the creation of Project Re:Wind. I'm incredibly grateful for her support and perspective.

The story is about people making choices under pressure and living with the outcomes of your actions whether you're ready or not. If any part of this story stuck with you after you closed the book, that means more to me than I can really put into words.

Thank you for spending time with it.

Scan to learn more about the world of Re:Wind.

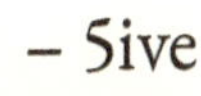

– 5ive